The Doggest
of Dog Days

A Seasonaire Story

M A CLARKE

First (and only) Edition

Published by Tekamutt Media 2015

Other books by the author:

Lunaria

www.lunarianovel.com

ISBN: 978-0-9929585-3-4

The following is a true story.

Everything contained within this book actually happened in a French mountain ski resort called Meribel.

It is chock full of lies, nudity, violence, beastiality, in-jokes and references to things that will make no sense to anyone who wasn't working for Skiworld in Meribel during the 2014/2015 winter season.

CONTENTS

Reader discretion is advised. Proceed at your own risk.

CHAPTER ONE

Once upon a time, Tom was at Folie Douce. Dancing on the table, surrounded by beautiful people and pumping choons, he had an epiphany: this was the best job in the world.

Then the sky above darkened. A swirling vortex of cloud appeared over the party, and a bright beam of blue light fell upon Tom as he gaped up at it with his mouth dangling wide.

"What is th—" he started, but suddenly he was floating upwards into the air. The DJ cranked it up, unaware of Tom's predicament, while others cheered at him, assuming this was part of an elaborate act.

He disappeared into the cloud and was gone.

Jack and Chris had seen the whole thing go down. They stood at the back, smoking a couple of rollups, which were hanging loose in their fingers. They stared at the spot in the sky where Tom had disappeared, unsure what to say.

Eventually, Jack broke the silence. "That was so dog, man."

CHAPTER TWO

Meanwhile, up in the DC Park, Hannah and Sophie were pulling 3's and twisting flipz and finishing off each other's sentences. So, a fairly average Tuesday afternoon.

Phil and Amy skidded down to stop in front of them.

"Shribs!" cried Hannah gleefully. All four of them put fists together in the middle, then punched towards the sky shouting "Team SHRIBLETS!" because that's probably what they do...

Afterwards, Amy gave them a concerned look. "Guys, you won't believe this, but I think there's a tiger eating people over there." She pointed up the slope, where stampede's of people were hurtling down from the Chatalet lift in a frenzy, all nearly colliding and cutting each other up.

Sophie frowned in confusion. "No, that run always looks like that."

But then the tiger appeared. Followed by a lion. It wasn't a snow tiger, it was a regular orange and black tiger, clearly lost because they don't usually like mountains and snow.

Phil gaped at the lion in awe, it reminded her of The Lion King, and she found herself fighting the urge to burst into a rendition of 'It's the Circle of Life.'

Then the big cats saw them all standing there, and

came charging towards them, great paws pounding up lumps of snow in their wake.

"AAAAIIIEEE!" the shriblets wailed, and fled down the mountain with the rest of the terrified tourists.

CHAPTER THREE

It was time for Gethin to do his evening shuttle rounds. He stepped out the front door of his luxury apartment, 'La Shack', and made his way to Astemy where the van was parked. He heard screams coming from inside, but he ignored them, because there were always screams coming from Chalet Astemy, and he knew better than to get involved.

He drove down the winding roads and pulled up next to the Chaudanne, ready to collect his guests. It was busier than usual, Geth noticed. And more… panicky. Crowds of skiers ran around in all directions, shouting and waving their hands. He had barely come to a stop when the sliding door flew open and twelve total strangers piled into the back seats. "DRIVE!!!" a man yelled in his ear.

"Who the fuck are you?" Geth responded, rightfully so. These were not Skiworld guests. How dare they get into his van?

A crazy woman opened his door, clambered into his lap and slammed her heavy ski boot onto the accelerator. The van lurched forwards and Geth fumbled to grab the steering wheel as the van skidded across the roundabout and flew into the tunnel heading for Mottaret. "What's going on!?" he cried with a mouthful of crazy lady's jumper.

"It ate her whole arm!" someone behind him yelled. "I saw it!"

"We have to get out of Meribel!" another shrieked.

"It ate her? What are you talking about!" Geth shouted. The van careened out of the tunnel and weaved up the icy road. Geth couldn't see where he was going, so he shoved the lady to the side, but her foot was still on the accelerator and he couldn't brake.

A car came flying towards him in the other direction. "*LOOK OUT!*"

SMASH! They collided with the car and the van jerked violently around as all the stupid strangers wailed in terror in the back seat and all Geth could do was wail back, "Why does this keep happening to meeeeeee!?"

CHAPTER FOUR

At Chalet Astemy, Laura was busy chopping potatoes, ready for the guests that would be home soon. Ricky strolled into the kitchen with sausages wedged onto his fingers and proceeded to jab them under Laura's chin in what may have been an attempted tickling.

"Get off!" she flinched, shoving him away. He held them up, wriggling the pork in her face.

"Do you like my meat gloves?"

"You could lay the table, you know?" she glared.

"Oh, all right." He sulked into the living room.

Soon after, Laura heard a *CRASH* followed by a yelp of surprise. "What have you done now?" she cried. She dropped the peeler and went to check on him. Ricky was stark-bollock naked, leaning out of the window clutching his trousers which were trying to fly away.

"The ghost stole my clothes!" he yelled in distress.

"What!?" Laura turned just in time to see the grinning spectral spirit swoop through her, stealing all of her clothes in the process. She screamed and ran after the bundle as another window opened by itself and slammed shut just as her Skiworld t-shirt flapped through it like a bird and took off into the sky.

Standing in the living room in their birthday suits, Ricky and Laura exchanged a worried look. "The guests will be home soon, what are we gonna do?!"

Then all of the doors in the chalet started opening

and slamming shut in a mad orchestra of chaos.

"Oh, not again…" they groaned.

CHAPTER FIVE

"GOLD!" shouted Fleur.

"GOLD!" yelled Hayley, pumping the air.

"ALWAYS BELIEVE IN YOUR SOOOOUL!" cried Immy at the top of her lungs.

They were in Jack's bar, dancing in front of The Elements, singing their song in mildly-intoxicated harmony. Dinner service was over, tomorrow was day off, and this was going to be a good night.

After another fourteen songs, Immy declared "It's too hot!" and strode outside for some air. Hayley and Fleur followed her into the road, where she was dancing under the stars with a frozen lamp post.

"Wheeee!" Immy sang as she went spinning around the lamp post. Then a dragon swooped down, plucked her up in its big green talons and flew away into the air. "Wheeee!" she went again, her gleeful cries echoing over the snowy slopes.

"Immy!" Fleur and Hayley stared in drunken disbelief at the big scaly creature as it flapped its leathery wings and soared across the valley. "It's flying to Mont Vallon! We need to save her!" Hayley raised a finger to emphasise her idea.

"Yes!" Fleur agreed, swaying on her feet a bit. "But it is very cold…"

"You're right," agreed Hayley. "We will save her tomorrow."

"We'll save you tomorrow, Immy!" Fleur yelled

into the sky.

"Okaaaay!" came Immy's faint reply, carried on the wind.

Fleur blinked. "Wow, she actually heard us."

They went back into Jack's and ordered a pizza, vowing to set off first thing in the morning to rescue their friend.

CHAPTER SIX

At Chez la Comtesse, a hundred miles from civilisation in the arse crack of the valley, Matt was waiting for his guests to come home to eat their stone-cold dinner.

"They are so late!" he pondered aloud. He was sitting at the table on his computer. "I wonder if they all got eaten by a tiger, or a lion, or a dragon? How completely unrealistic and ridiculous would that be? Who would even think of that?"

He realised he was talking to an empty room again.

Whatever the reason, his lack of guests meant that he was free to carry on writing. He could sit here and make up whatever random shite he felt like all night long, which to be honest was how he always worked anyway…

CHAPTER SEVEN

Sue was in her apartment, busily counting up all of Skiworld's profits for the day, and cackling maniacally to herself. She liked to cackle while counting Skiworld's money, but only when nobody was looking.

Steph burst in through the door carrying a stack of toilet rolls. "Can you believe it!?" she cried.

Sue quickly turned the cackle into a hacking cough to disguise her secret evil laughter. Steph went on, oblivious. "Super-U have given us nineteen boxes of loo roll as a replacement for sugar!" She slung the toilet rolls across the room. "What am I supposed to do with this lot!?"

Sue raised her eyebrows and shrugged. Steph planted both hands on her hips and stared at the heap. "By the way, have you heard from Tom? Apparently, he disappeared after après and no one's seen him since. I swear if anything else goes wrong today, I'm gonna kill someone!"

"Maybe the dragon took him?" Sue suggested. "Or the tigers."

"What are you talking about?"

"Yeah, the resorts gone completely mental. I'm staying out of it 'til it all blows over."

"Screw it," Steph declared. "It's day off tomorrow, and nothing's gonna stop me going out, not even a bloody dragon." She went into her bedroom to get changed and closed the door.

Sue turned back to her pile of coins. "Mwhahaha," she chuckled quietly.

The door opened, "What did you say?" Steph asked.

"Nothing!"

CHAPTER EIGHT

The night was cold, still, and full of stars. A full moon shone over the snowy landscape, painting the trees a dull shade of grey. Somewhere in the valley, a wolf howled, its mournful song echoing off the mountains.

A stubble-faced man listened to it as he stalked along the icy road. He wore a trenchcoat and wide brimmed hat pulled down over his face, making his way towards the scene of the accident. *Accident*, he thought to himself. *Yeah, right*. He knew the scent of murder, and this night reeked of it.

He'd snuck away from Jack's Bar, where all his colleagues were busy drinking and having fun. He had bigger fish to fry tonight. He came upon the upside down van in a ditch beside the road, surrounded by police tape. Gazing at the crumpled wreckage, it was no wonder Gethin didn't make it out alive.

Gethin was just the latest victim in a string of mysterious unsolved cases that he'd taken upon himself to solve.

First, there was Josh. Official report said he'd gone to VT, but no-one had seen him since. Then there was Kate and Kenny, both disappeared without a trace. Then Max, choked on one of his own cakes, poor sod. Or was he poisoned...? And now, Gethin. Who would be next?

He studied the scene, and noticed a set of skid marks leading away from the collision point. A car had been coming the other way, at deadly speed. He bent to study the tyre marks. A hatchback, he guessed. Something small and nippy. Ideal getaway car.

"I'll find you, Seasonaire Serial Killer," he vowed, clenching a fist. "…if it's the last thing I do."

He heard the screech of tyres, and a flash of headlights lit up the road. He jolted around to see a car veering towards him. He dived and rolled out of the way. The car sped over his hat, crushing it into the ice before speeding up the hill and out of sight.

It was a small car, just as he suspected. It looked silver, but he couldn't be sure - everything looked silver in the glow of the moonlight. He shook his fist at the tail lights. "Thought you had me, didn't you! But it takes more than that to kill Detective Ollie Bennet!" He realised he was shouting and gazed around nervously making sure nobody had heard or seen him. He tugged the collar up to hide his face, and stalked back to town. Better to rejoin the others before anybody noticed his absence.

He'd danced with death tonight, and lived to tell the tale. Time for a stiff drink while he considered his next move…

CHAPTER NINE

Arooooooooooooo!

"Did you hear that!?" Sophie cried, frantically poling the powdery snow.

"Was that a wolf?" Amy blurted, feeling very distressed as she pumped her tired little arms.

"Never mind the wolf," said Hannah, overtaking them both. "That lion's still behind us!"

"Please leave us alone, Mr. Lion," Philly despaired, bringing up the rear.

"What about the tiger?" Amy said with wide eyes darting left and right. "Where's the tiger gone?!"

"It ran off into the trees!" Phil called.

"Whose idea was it to come into this stupid forest, anyway?" Sophie snapped.

"Yours!" they all replied at once.

"*Roar!*" went the lion.

"*Aiiiee!*"

They emerged from the trees in a clearing, and spotted a ramshackle wooden hut with strangely glowing colourful windows.

"We can hide in there!" Amy pointed.

They skied as fast as they could towards the hut. The tiger leapt out from the trees in front of them. "TIGER!" they wailed. "We're trapped!"

Suddenly, the door to the hut burst open and a man wielding a disco ball and lasers came out, cheering and dancing. At the sight of the strange man, both the tiger and lion froze in their tracks, wary of the dazzling light show and pumping music that blared out of the hut.

The shriblets didn't waste time wondering what this man was doing out here by himself. They raced right up to the door and flew into the hut, landing in a messy heap of skis, poles and tangled hair.

The tiger charged at the disco man but he calmly stepped inside and slammed the door on its face. He turned to the shriblets and grinned. "Welcome to the party!" They could barely hear him over the sound of the sub-woofer. "Don't worry, those kitty cats won't bother us in here, so long as we're funking it up!"

"Woohoo!" cried the girls, punching fists awkwardly into the air.

Then the power cut out and everything went dark.

CHAPTER TEN

"So you're telling me that Tom just floated off into the sky?" Ben asked Chris. They were sitting round a table in Jack's Bar.

"Yeah man, exactly," Chris nodded, downing the rest of his beer. "I'm not even joking."

Ben scoffed. "How much did you and Jack have to drink?"

Chris said defensively, "Nothing, man!" He frowned. "Well, maybe a couple."

Jack slumped down at the table with three fresh pints. "Chris man, stop telling everyone about that. People will think we're crazy."

"Yeah I s'pose…" Chris mumbled. "But I know what I saw."

Ollie stopped at the table on his way to the bar. He was covered in snow.

Jack pointed and said, "What happened to you?"

"Nothing." Ollie quickly changed the subject. "Guys, do you know anyone who drives a small silver car?"

"I think Sue does," Ben replied.

"Reeeeally?" Ollie pinched his chin between thumb and forefinger, and peered across the room at Sue with narrow eyes.

"Why?" Ben asked, frowning.

Ollie didn't reply. He just kept eyeing Sue with a suspicious gaze for some reason. She noticed, and waved cheerily from across the room. The wait for him to respond became embarrassingly long. "Okaaaay," she said, turning back to Steph, who was engaged in a heated argument about whether the barman needed any extra toilet rolls.

CHAPTER ELEVEN

Fleur and Hayley bundled over and joined the others at the table, armed with a steaming pizza. They immediately started stuffing slices into their mouths.

"Easy girls," Ben said. "You in a hurry to be somewhere?"

"Yesht," Fleur said, chewing. "We hasf to safe Immy fwom tha dragon."

"But firsht," Hayley added. "We need to eats schomething and then shleep."

"A dragon?!" Ben exclaimed. First tigers, lions, then floating Tom's, now a dragon? "My resort's going to shit!" he cried. "I'm not having it. I've dealt with grumbling guests, spoilt kids and that one punter each week who leaves ketchup on the edge of the plate at breakfast, squelching in my fingers as I try to clean up and I won't take it anymore!"

What was a dragon, compared to all that? Besides, he couldn't let Fleur face it alone. "I'm coming too." He turned to Jack and Chris, "You in, boys?"

"Nah," Jack said. "Sounds like effort."

"Mmmm," Chris nodded agreement, swigging his pint. He was eyeing a cute brunette at the bar.

"Looks like it's down to me," Ben declared, slamming a fist on the table. "I'll lead us then, girls. I'll find us a shortcut to the beast's lair!"

"Okay!" Hayley and Fleur said together as cheese dangled from their chins.

And with that, the Meribel Dragon Hunter's Association was formed.

CHAPTER TWELVE

Wednesday had finally arrived.

Alex awoke early, bright and fresh, ready to face the day. He tore open the curtains and declared to the sky, "Good morning, world!" He put on his jacket, his helmet, pulled the goggles down over his head, and grabbed his snowboard. He strode out the door and caught the lift right to the top of the mountain.

The sun shone across a bright blue, cloudless sky. Alex boarded down the empty slopes amid a glorious backdrop of pristine peaks as far as the eye could see. As he soared, he knew this was what it felt like to be truly free and alive. A small tear fell from the corner of his eye at the pure, undeniable happiness of it all.

What I'm trying to say is Alex was doing exactly what he does every day.

Brring brring! The magnificent peace was interrupted by his work phone ringing out of his pocket.

"Ignore it!" Alex's beard said gruffly.

"But it might be important!" he replied, his face turning sad.

"Fuck 'em!" his beard insisted. "It'll be a broken light bulb, or some guest with his finger stuck in a plughole again! Let 'em hang!"

Alex sighed. "Okay, beard. You always do know what's best."

"Only looking out for you, boss man."

On the other end of the phone, Ricky was trapped in the bathroom where the ghost had locked him in. "Alex, why won't you answer?? I *NEED* YOU!"

CHAPTER THIRTEEN

Andy jolted awake and banged his head on something hard. "Ow." He blinked a few times until his surroundings came into focus. "Oh, no. Where am I?"

He seemed to be in a tiny wooden house, covered in hairs and smelling of dog. *Woof!* He looked out of the kennel, and saw a big shaggy pooch lying on his belly, wagging a happy tail.

"Oh god, this is a first," Andy grumbled. When he tried to stand up, his arm gave a painful twang. "Yow!" he flinched. It didn't feel broken, but it didn't feel that good either.

He decided to ignore it. That decision worked out fine the last time, after all.

Crawling out of the kennel, he staggered to his feet and searched about. Wooden chalet's rose up around him, some five stories high. He had no idea where he was or how he got there.

He showed the dog both of his index fingers. "Stay," he said. He backed away slowly and wandered out onto the road. A few skiers were waiting for a bus in the morning sun. They noticed him and called out, "Hey! What happened to your clothes? You look like you lost a fight with a bear!"

Andy looked down, and realised all of his clothes were ripped and hanging off him in shreds. *Did I get mauled by a bear last night?* He pondered. He uttered a nervous laugh and shrugged at the people, before stumbling on down the hill.

He hoped he might find his way back to his apartment, and some breakfast. Yes, some bacon would make everything feel better. After that, he could figure out what happened last night...

CHAPTER FOURTEEN

High atop the summit of Mont Vallon, the morning sun stirred Immy back into consciousness. She yawned, smiling sleepily. That was one of the most comfortable night's sleep she had ever had. It was so warm and cozy here in this…nest?

Her eyes widened and she looked around in some considerable shock.

"Where am I?" she asked herself. There was straw all around her, an Immy-shaped flat section where she had been laying. "Wow, I do not remember climbing up here." She scratched the back of her head.

Then she noticed the 3 giant eggs in the nest with her. They were as big as she was. "Wooooow," she cooed. She reached out and touched one, feeling its warm, waxy shell.

Crack!

A horizontal split appeared around the egg she was touching. She leaned back to watch, filled with curiosity. A scaly green head, wearing the top of the eggshell like a hat, lifted up and looked at her. It had big cute yellow eyes, slitted like a cat's.

"Hello!" Immy said, waving. The baby dragon licked its lips, and showed her a row of tiny, pointed teeth. "Look at you!" Immy reached out to pet him on the nose, but it went *CHOMP*! Immy flinched away just in time. "That's naughty!" she scolded it, and slapped him on the nose.

The baby dragon yelped and cowered back inside his egg.

"Aw, I'm sorry. Why don't you...wait a second. You're a French dragon." Immy cleared her throat. "Bonjour. Je m'apelle Immy. Et tu?"

The baby did not respond for some time. Immy tried to think of something else to say in French, but suddenly, the other two eggs hatched at the same time, and two more squealing baby dragons flopped about in the straw flapping their tiny little wings. The first one reappeared, looking up at the sky and yapping.

Immy clapped her hands, excited. "You're all so cute!"

Then a massive shadow fell across the nest, and something huge landed behind her in the snow. The baby dragons screeched for joy, looking past Immy at whatever was behind her.

Slowly, she turned around. "Oh. Hello..."

CHAPTER FIFTEEN

Tom opened his eyes and found himself looking in a mirror. *Oh, what a handsome fellow*, he thought to himself. Then his reflection spoke to him, and he realised it wasn't a mirror at all. It was an exact copy of himself.

"Greetings, The Tom!" His not-reflection spread palms and smiled happily at him.

"Wha…?" Tom said, very confused. He looked around the strange circular room made entirely out of white glass. Through the window, he could see the Earth in space, surrounded by stars.

Standing in the room with him were over a dozen more Tom's. One of them said, "You have returned to us!"

Tom was speechless. He covered his eyes with a hand. "Oh, god, I swear I didn't drink that much…"

"Is The Tom okay?"

"He looks troubled."

"Must be the altitude."

"Yes, probably."

Tom shook his head. "What are you on about? Who are you, and why do you all look exactly like me?"

The first Tom gave him a quizzical look. "You are The Tom, our leader. Don't you remember us? We have been watching you, as you mingled with the humans to learn their ways, so as to bring valuable knowledge back to our home, Par-Tay."

"We have learned much from you, oh Wise One!" another Tom declared.

"You taught us the art of making strangers believe you care about them."

"And how to dance on top of a table without spilling your beer!"

Tom started to smile. He couldn't remember being their leader, but it was somehow starting to make sense.

"Yes!" another one added, "and you showed us how to backflip over a snow jump and smash your head in front of friends!"

Tom frowned. "Err, yes. Of course I did."

"So, are you ready to return to planet Par-Tay, across the galaxy?"

Tom considered that. "Is that where you... I mean, we, all come from?"

"Yes!"

"Hmm," he said, rubbing his chin thoughtfully. He looked out of the window at planet Earth, slowly spinning. "But I kinda like it down there. Can I say bye to my friends first?"

Another Tom said, "Of course. But you better be quick. Last we saw, a few of them were being chased by some unsavoury-looking cats."

"I must help them!" Tom decided, stepping into a teleporter chamber. "I will return soon, brothers!"

"I'm your sister, actually," a Tom said with a cheeky wave. Tom frowned.

The other Tom's saluted, but one of them panicked shouting, "Hurry, The Tom! We must depart in two—" But Tom's head started spinning *zzzzoooooooooommmm*! And he disappeared.

CHAPTER SIXTEEN

"Naaaaaah…" Matt said aloud as he finished typing the latest chapter. Tom, an alien? That was a bit far-fetched. But then the hint was right there in the very first chapter. I mean, how else was he going to explain Tom randomly floating up into the sky? Maybe drunkenly starting a story before having the slightest idea of where it would lead wasn't his smartest move. No forward planning, that was the mistake…

But he was committed now, there was no alternative but to steamroll ahead. So, Tom was from another planet and had magical party powers or something and he'd have to go with it, even if people started to think he was mental for writing such a ridiculous tale that made no sense.

Where were we?

Oh, yes.

"AAAAAIIIIIEEE!" screamed Laura as all of her frying pans flew around the room like angry metal bats. They clanged off the walls and each other and dive-bombed her as she swatted at them with a frozen bag of bacon. "Ricky, get in here!"

Ricky and his fringe skidded through the door, armed with a pair of rubber gloves and a mop. "The ghost!" he pointed at the flying cooking utensils. "The ghost must be doing that!"

Laura curled her lip in disbelief. "You think?! Help

me stop it before it wakes all the guests up!"

The frying pans seemed to sense their intent, and all flew out of the kitchen into the living room. Ricky and Laura charged after them. He flailed the mop above his head, swiping at the pans.

Laura struck one with the frozen bacon and it made a loud *DONG*. All of the frying pans froze in midair. Then two of them clanged against each other, mimicking the sound, *DONG!*

"Oh no…" Laura said.

The other frying pans joined in, hammering into each other again and again.

DONG! CLANG! BONG! BOOM! BING! GONG! BANG!

Laura and Ricky covered their ears and looked helplessly at each other against the onslaught of musical haunted frying pans.

Without warning, the pans all suddenly went dead and clattered to the floor, bouncing around until finally silence settled over the chalet.

Slowly, they removed their hands from their ears and looked nervously about. "Thank god," Laura said.

"I've just about had enough of this," Ricky added. "We need to deal with this ghost once and for all."

"What the hell are you two doing!?"

They turned around to see a man in his dressing gown staring at the sea of saucepans in utter confusion. He was a guest.

Ricky stood up straight and waved.

"Um," Laura said. She forced her brightest smile. "Would you like some porridge?"

CHAPTER SEVENTEEN

"Let's go save Immy!" Fleur cried, raising both hands in the air. They were at Mottaret, standing by the snowman statue. Usually, crowds of people milled about, but today it was eerily empty, and none of the lifts were running.

Hayley gazed at the summit of Mont Vallon in the distance. "Do you think Immy is all right?" She chewed her lip. "Maybe we should have gone straight away, instead of, you know, eating pizza and going to sleep."

Fleur looked at her, opened her mouth to say something, but she couldn't think of an answer to that.

"Also," Hayley pointed at a dormant bubble lift. "How are we supposed to get there if the lifts aren't working?"

Ben marched past, wearing an explorer's hat and pointing at the mountain with a cane. "We have to hike! This way!"

"Where did you get that from?" Fleur asked, happy with the distraction. She scurried after him.

Hayley took a deep breath and followed them into the valley.

"Hey! Wait a-for me!"

They turned around and saw Luca running across the snow towards them.

He was twirling a pizza dough above his head, and

a camera swung to and fro from his neck. He came to a panting stop in front of them, and tossed the pizza dough high into the air. "I hear about a dragon!" His thick Italian accent made it very difficult to understand what he was saying. "I can help you to a-slay the monster, yes! And I will a-document the adventure with my veedeo camera!" He pointed to the camera with one hand and caught the pizza dough with the other, instantly twirling it again.

"Have you ever fought a dragon before?" Ben squinted at him. "Do you know what we're up against?"

"Ah!" Luca casually danced with the pizza dough. "You mean the razor sharp teeth, and the claws like deadly spears, and the breath of fire that burns the flesh from your bones, yes? Yes! I have defeated many a dragons in my country."

Ben shrugged. "Sounds good to me. You're in." He pointed at the mountain and began marching again. "Onward!"

Fleur and Hayley hadn't really given a lot of thought to the specifics of the dragon, until now. They hugged each other, gaping at Luca in terror.

Luca just gaped back at the girls, the sight so distracting that he almost dropped the dough. He recovered by disguising the fumble as another throw, and lobbed it into the air. "Lesbian action!" He thumped a fist against his chest. "I'm in the right place."

The pizza dough splatted on his head.

CHAPTER INFINITY

Time stood still in Meribel. The tiger froze mid-swipe at the cabin door while the Shriblets cowered in the dark within. Ricky and Laura stood like statues in the living room, shielding their faces from an onslaught of possessed napkins. Jack and Chris slept. Luca's pizza base hovered above his fingers, while Ben and the girls froze mid-stride in knee-deep snow. Andy scratched his head, followed by a curious pack of dogs.

And Julia rested in a hospital bed. She's not with Skiworld, but she might as well be. She puts in more effort keeping The Shack tidy than the rest of its inhabitants combined. She may not be Skiworld, but she is one of us. And today, some arsehole broke her back.

The thing is, danger can come when you least expect it. Be it a ravenous tiger, a hungry dragon, a really annoying ghost, or an out of control idiot on the piste - it doesn't matter how good you are, sometimes things happen that are beyond our control. All we can do is look out for each other, and wear a goddamn helmet Ricky Payne.

Jules, our thoughts are with you tonight.

CHAPTER EIGHTEEN

Jack and Chris had slept in. They didn't mean to, but it had been one of those long nights that ended in Sullies and bed at 5am, the usual Tuesday night ordeal. Since today was their day off, neither was too keen on leaving the comfort of their duvet. Or, in Chris's case, his juvet.

Jack pried his eyes open and squinted at the sunshine pouring through the window. He groaned, and staggered out of bed to take a piss. "Oi, Chris! We slept in on a blue bird, man."

Chris responded with an incomprehensible grumble.

Jack flushed the toilet, preened his eyebrows in the mirror, and then went to get changed.

An hour later, they stepped off the bus in the Chaudanne and looked about. It was deserted.

"Where is everyone?" Chris pondered.

"I dunno," Jack replied." None of the lifts are moving. Think there's been a powercut?"

"It's all *BESSIE's FAULT!*"

Jack and Chris both jumped, and turned around to see who was yelling at them. They came face to face with a man balancing on a unicycle, juggling skittles.

"What the fuuuck?" Jack said, frowning.

"Hello," said the juggler. "Have you seen Bessie?"

Chris laughed. "What you on about? We don't know anyone called Bessie."

"Ohhhh," the juggler groaned, his face full of sadness. "She escaped yesterday and I haven't been able to find her. She ate people!"

Jack screwed up his face. "Who eats people? That's well wrong."

"Yeah, she shouldn't do that," Chris agreed.

"Well, she can't help it, can she!" wailed the juggler, still juggling. "She's a lion!"

"This place is going mental," Chris mumbled to Jack.

"Yeah, I know." Jack turned to the juggler. "Well, see ya!" He waved and they turned to walk away.

"Help me find her!" the juggler called.

"Nah man, we wanna go skiing."

"I'll pay you!"

They stopped. Turned around.

"How much?"

The juggler caught his skittles, and stepped off the unicycle. He reached into a pocket and held out a big wad of notes in a fan.

Jack and Chris gazed at the money with wide eyes and drooping mouths. "Woooah," they both said together.

CHAPTER NINETEEN

Woof!

"Go away!" Andy shooed the dogs for the fifth time, but they just kept following him. As he rounded the corner, heading down the hill, somewhere towards town, another one joined the pack behind him.

Woof! Seven pooches now, including one particularly big shaggy thing that seemed to enjoy burying his nose up Andy's butt whenever he turned around.

"Get off!" Andy yelped, picking up his pace.

The dogs followed, all scurrying along, sniffing and peeing on lamp posts to mark their passage.

He spied some people coming the other way up the hill, so Andy instinctively ducked behind a bin to hide. He'd had enough of people commenting on his torn clothes, and still couldn't remember how he got in such a state.

The dogs all padded over and crowded around the bin, looking at him with their tongues hanging out.

"Shh!" Andy said with a finger over his lips. He could hear the people coming now, they were talking.

"…it was huge!" one man said.

"I know. It came out of nowhere and started fighting the lion. It saved everyone!"

"What do you think it was?"

"I dunno…a werewolf?"

They both snorted in laughter as they passed by Andy's bin.

"As if. Werewolves don't exist."

"It could be though! It was a full moon last night."

"Yeah but come on, do you know how cra…"

Then they were too far away for Andy to hear.

A werewolf? he thought to himself.

Something prodded his arse again and he gave a shrill cry. "Will you stop doing that!" he scolded the big shaggy dog.

Woof! the dog replied, but somehow Andy heard 'Alpha!'

He blinked. "Did you just speak…?"

'Alpha!' the dog woofed again.

Then all the dogs rolled onto their backs, showing their bellies. A sign of submission.

"Oh god…" Andy looked around, hoping nobody else was seeing this.

He decided to leave the road, hopped over a fence and waded through the snow down the hill.

All of the dogs bounded after him, yipping and woofing, but all Andy heard was 'Alpha! Alpha! Alpha!'

CHAPTER TWENTY

"Hey, boss man?"

"Yes, beard?"

"I got a joke for you."

Alex stopped tightening the nut underneath the leaky sink, and sighed. "Not again, beard."

It ignored Alex's lack of enthusiasm. "Why do the French only have one egg for breakfast?"

Alex drooped his head. "I don't know beard, why?"

"Because un ouef is enough!"

Alex didn't respond.

"You can laugh now, boss man."

"I know. It's just…you've told me that joke every day for the last seventeen weeks."

"Maybe you don't get it," his beard explained. "You see, 'un ouef' sounds like 'enough.'"

"Yeah…"

A silence lingered for some time.

"It doesn't quite work when it's written down," his beard admitted.

"That's it, I'm getting the razor." Alex crawled out from under the sink.

"What? To kill yourself? The joke isn't *THAT* bad."

"No, beard! Don't be so morose! I'm shaving you off."

His beard went tight. All his beardy hairs bristled

and he got angry. "WHAT? YOU CAN'T!"

"Yes I can."

"But you won't."

Alex stopped. "Why not?"

"Because what sort of self-respecting handyman would you be without a glorious chin-mane?"

Alex considered that. "Hmm…you're right."

"Damn right I'm right."

"Aww, thanks beard. You saved me from doing something silly again."

"Always here for you, boss man. Now, come 'ere."

And Alex and his beard sloppily started making out with each other and everyone reading was stuck trying to imagine what that looked like.

CHAPTER TWENTY-ONE

Steph burst out of her room armed with a bow and arrow. "That's it! I've had *ENOUGH* of Brake, and Super-U, and the whole bloody lot."

Sue raised an eyebrow. "What's happened now?"

"They've only run out of venison! What are the signature guests supposed to think if we can't serve them fresh venison!?" She spread her arms wide as if the solution was obvious. "Come on, we're going hunting. Sue, get your crossbow."

"How do you know I have a crossbow?" Sue said, alarmed.

Steph put a hand on her hip. "I've seen it under your pillow. Come on, you're driving."

They piled an assortment of hunting gear into the back of Sue's car, and jumped in. Sue drove them down the hill and out of town, but somewhere between Nantgerel and Les Allues, the engine started to sputter, and then conked out completely.

"What?" Sue frowned at her dashboard. "Out of petrol!?"

"Didn't you fill up?"

"Yes! Yesterday!" How had she ran out so quickly? "Has someone been using my car?" Sue said, eyeing Steph suspiciously.

"Don't look at me!" Steph said. She peered out of the window. "This'll do, anyway. There's bound to be some deer in those trees."

Before Sue could argue, Steph jumped out and started pulling her weapons from the boot.

Sue grabbed her crossbow, adjusted her bobble hat and followed Steph into the deep snow.

On the roof of the car, Detective Ollie dropped down and hid behind a wheel. Luckily for him, the girls had been too preoccupied with stuffing grenades into their pockets to notice him. He watched their backs with deep suspicion. "What nefarious deeds are you up to now, Sue…?" he mused, rubbing his stubbly chin. "Could Steph be your next victim?" He glanced left and right to make sure no-one was watching, pulled up his collar and stalked into the trees behind them.

CHAPTER TWENTY-TWO

Hannah, wearing nothing but a bra and salopettes, swung the axe as hard as she could, aiming for the tiny little cork.

She hit poor Phil instead.

How it came to this, no-one could tell. Playing strip-axe-cork-chopping had seemed like a good way to pass the time in the dark party cabin, but considering there was a tiger clawing at the door outside, and the power cut made it pitch black inside, someone was bound to get hurt eventually.

And Phil's time had come...

She tumbled into Amy's arms, who clutched her friend, staring into each other's eyes.

"Farewell Amy..." Phil choked, bleeding from her axe wound. "...until we meet again..."

"Phil!" Amy cried.

But Phil was gone.

There was no time to weep, for just then, a mighty crash filled the room, and daylight flooded the cabin.

"ROAR!" went the tiger, prowling through the smashed door and into the cabin.

"The tiger!" the surviving shriblets shrieked at once. Sophie and Hannah hugged each other tight, fearing the end.

Amy held poor Phil in her arms as the tiger made its move.

It reared up on hind legs, and raised a massive paw

in the air, about to swipe. It reached out, aiming for Amy's head…and suddenly, it froze. Its out-stretched paw held steady.

And then the lasers started. Booming music pumped out of the speakers. A figure had appeared in the doorway, too shadowy to see their face, but a familiar voice cried out, "PAR-TAY!"

And the tiger started doing the Macarena.

CHAPTER TWENTY-THREE

Matt, I mean, New Matt, the good-looking one who took over Geth's job as driver, despite it technically only being a single night since his fateful death in the story but more like 3 or 4 weeks in something called real life......was queueing for a chair lift.

Somehow, Matt had found the one lift that was still running, and every punter left in resort was at Morel trying to get onto it.

He casually spied a couple of hotties in the line behind him, and decided to sit with them. So, he let people cut in front of him in the line, studied the trees, and looked around feigning frustration, as if his 'friends' were late, until eventually the two girls caught up to him in the queue.

Smooooothly done, he congratulated himself.

Then a man slammed a ski pole into his foot.

It didn't hurt, since Matt was wearing ski boots, but the menacing look in the man's eyes told him all he needed to know: *Don't even think about it, sonny.*

It was probably the girls' father... Defeated, Matt let them pass, then got onto the next chair.

"Well hellooo there!" a female voice said to his left. He looked over and saw two even HOTTER females had joined him. They spoke with a strange Lebanese accent. Matt couldn't believe his luck. The chair lifted them off the ground and began their slow ascent to the top. Plenty of time for Matt to get his charm on.

"Greetings, ladies, how are we today?" He beamed.

"Ugh!" They wrinkled their nose. "What is that SMELL? Have you been eating garlic?"

"Umm…maybe."

"You could kill a vampire with that breath!"

Matt turned sad. His addiction to eating whole bulbs of garlic had finally caught up to him.

"My apologies, ladies." And with that, he raised the bar of the lift and leapt out, doing a casual backflip, followed by a twist and landed in the snow perfectly to ski away through the trees.

The Lebanese girls stared after him. "Wow!"

But it was too late, Garlic Matt was on his way to his unexpected future appearance in the story.

CHAPTER TWENTY-FOUR

"Are you sure this is going to work?" Laura asked nervously.

"Yes, 100%," Ricky assured her, ushering her into the tiny Hobbit room. Inside, a miniature table and chairs were set up, with a Ouija board and some candles arranged on it. "Sit down and start chanting."

"I don't want to!" Laura insisted. "What if the ghost gets angry?"

"That's the whole point!" Ricky said. "Just chant and sing and whatever until it shows up, then I'll zap it!" He held up the home-made Ghostbusters plasma rifle that he had fashioned out of a hoover nozzle, the innards of the microwave and a Brad sack.

Laura didn't look convinced that it was going to work, but she sat down anyway and looked at the Ouija board. "Um…hello, Mr. Ghost… Are you there?"

"What kind of ritualistic séance chanting do you call that?" Ricky said, peering in from outside the Hobbit room. "Do this: hnnnnggg, ummmmnggggg, hubba hooba hunga mungo *woooooooooomb*." He was pulling strange faces and jiggling his hands as he chanted gibberish noises.

Laura was just about to give it a try for herself, when one of the candles blew out. A shadow filled the room, spilling from the corners and spreading up the walls and across the ceiling.

"Um, Ricky…"

The other candles flickered against a cold breeze, even though the windows were all shut.

Ricky froze mid-chant, standing on one leg with his palms pressed together above his head. His eyes flicked about the room, watching the strange shadow crawling over the walls and across the floor.

"Ricky, I'm scared!" Laura shouted. She got up and ran for the door, but some invisible force dragged her back inside. "Aiieee!" she shrieked.

Ricky aimed and fired.

A colourful burst of sparks shot out of his homemade proton gun, immediately disintegrating the curtains.

Laura started laughing, suspended in mid-air. Then she spoke, but it wasn't her voice. "Mwhaha you think you can harm me with that feeble contraption? I've possessed your girlfriend! What are you going to do about it?!" the ghost mocked.

Ricky aimed at Laura and fired without hesitation.

"Oww!" Laura yelped. The ghost let her go and she fell to the floor with a bump. "Ricky, stop shooting me!"

"Sorry," he said, still aiming the gun at her just in case. The shadow disappeared and the room had gone quiet. "Did we kill it?"

Laura looked about, rubbing her sore head. "I hope so."

A faint scratching could be heard. It took a while for Ricky to notice where it was coming from, then his eyes fell upon the Ouija board, covered in little Scrabble letters. The letters were moving, forming a sentence…

Ricky gulped, pointed to the table, and they both

slowly crept towards it to read what the message said.

D-A-N-G-E-R

F-R-O-M

A-B-O-V-E

Ricky and Laura both looked up straight away, fearing some calamity from the ceiling. But there was nothing there.

"Danger from above?" Ricky said, frowning.

"What could it mean?" Laura asked.

But before they could think of anything, the ghost gave them horrendous wedgies and left them both dangling on some hooks in the boot room.

"How are we going to explain this to the guests?" Ricky squeaked.

CHAPTER TWENTY-FIVE

Mont Vallon rose up, piercing the sky with its grand snowy peak, the highest point in the whole of Meribel.

Four ragged travelers approached its foot, just by the abandoned lift station: two weary girls, an enthusiastic guide and a weirdo tossing a pizza.

Fleur could hardly breathe. "Are we there yet?"

"Not far now!" Ben declared, pointing at the top of the mountain, and marching relentlessly through the snow.

"I'm knackered," Hayley panted. "Immy better appreciate what we're doing for her."

Just then, a mighty screech echoed across the skies, and a huge black shape flapped its wings and took off from the summit. It soared away disappearing behind the mountain.

Fleur and Hayley both stared at the empty sky after it and gulped.

"The dragon has gone!" Ben cried. "We must hurry!" He cut a path into the deep snow, aiming to hike right up the side of the mountain.

"Wait a-for Luca! He will strike with a Margarita special!" The two boys strode away.

Hayley looked at the frozen lift and had a better idea. "Fleur, this way."

They walked past the chalk board sign that said 'CLOSED DUE TO DRAGON. GO HOME.' and walked into the lift station.

A sleepy man stirred when they approached. "Non! Non, non, non, c'est ferme!" He waved them away.

Hayley walked right up to him and crossed her arms. "Turn it on. I am not walking any further, so whether you like it or not, we are getting on this lift."

He didn't speak English, but he understood Hayley's firm tone and mean frown.

"Ooh la la, c'est tu funérailles." He pressed a big green button and the lift hummed to life.

The two girls jumped into a gondola and started their ascent.

"Yes Hayley," Fleur beamed. "That was awesome!" They high fived.

Down below, they saw the two boys struggling through the snow, and opened the window to shout, "See you at the top!"

Then they turned to look towards the peak of the mountain. "Immy, we're coming for you."

CHAPTER TWENTY-SIX

Jack and Chris had asked in every bar in town, looking for the lion, but nobody knew anything useful. Chris was getting annoyed. This whole thing was taking too long, the unicycling juggler was getting on his nerves, and they were running out of bars. Finally, at Rond Point, they found a lead, though.

"I seen yer lion!" cried a drunken old skier. "Last night! *HUGE* brawl, there were! I was 'ere, drinking my - *hiccup* - pint, and along comes this ravage hairy beast!"

Jack rubbed his chin. He whispered to Chris. "This guy's clearly hammered. He probably saw that big shaggy dog that hangs around here."

"A dog!" the drunk man cried. "Aye! There was a huge dog fighting the lion, fearsome as a wolf! He – *burp* - came out and fought with the lion. Terrible scrap, it were. Claws, and teeth... and biting and - *hiccup*-...." He lost his train of thought and dozed off.

"What happened to the lion, man?" Chris jabbed him in the ribs. "We need to find it."

The man jolted awake and squinted at Chris as if he had only just noticed he was there. "Say, you got a sister? I seen a girl just like you before... oooh, she were tasty. Really tall, wearing hot pants, and big knockers!" He jiggled his own man-boobs in emphasis. "You look just like her."

"Um, no... dunno nothin' about that, mate," Chris

scratched the back of his head.

"Where did the lion go?" Jack asked.

The man was still eyeing Chris, and licked his lips. "What?"

"The lion!" Jack repeated, on the brink of giving up.

The drunk man clicked his fingers and slapped his own head. "I remember a lion! I saw it last night!" He burped again. "The circus man took him away."

"Nooooo!" shrieked the juggler.

Chris and Jack winced at the horrible noise. "What's wrong now?" they asked.

"The circus is always stealing my lions!" He was still balancing on his unicycle and juggling, but now he was somehow doing both in an angry manner. "Come on! I know where those bastard clowns hang out." He rode away, still furiously juggling.

Chris shook his head. "Jack, what the fuck have we gotten ourselves into?"

"I dunno man, this is so dog. Let's just go and get our money."

CHAPTER TWENTY-SEVEN

Woof! Rowl! Raw! Ruff ruff! Yipp yap bark howl wooof!!

Andy and his pack of dogs, which had grown to about 30 noisy pooches now, came barging out of the forest and into the road, just outside Nantgerel.

"That's Matt's chalet!" Andy cried, and ran up the steps and into the kitchen slamming the door on the dogs' noses. "Peace, at last…"

Matt looked up from his writing. "Andy? What are you doing here?"

"I'm trying to get home! I'm starving and these dogs keep chasing me. It's so mule, man."

"Want some bacon?" Matt offered.

And they ate bacon. It was glorious.

Afterwards, Matt sat back down, staring at his screen with a crazy look in his eye and nearly pulling his hair out.

"You look stressed," Andy commented, which was funny coming from the man who had been running from a pack of dogs for 2 hours and who's clothes were dangling off him in threads.

"It's the story!" Matt cried. "It's getting away from me. There's dragons, ghosts, tigers, lions, crazy jugglers, a murder mystery and so many *CHARACTERS*, how is it all going to come together?!"

Andy put his hands out. "Take it easy, man. Just chill oooout." When he said 'out', it seemed to last a long time.

"Did you just howl at me?" Matt frowned.

"Err, no." Andy blinked. He did and he knew it. But he had no idea why. "I just said chill ooooooooooooooooout!"

"You did! You just howled again!"

Andy laughed nervously. "I think I better go."

He hastily left the room and went back outside, where all of the dogs started yipping and barking and howling and woofing and all of the urges that Andy had been resisting all day long failed him, and he let them take over. Hair sprouted across his body, his nose extended into a snout, and his senses exploded until he could smell and hear everything so much stronger, and suddenly he found himself on all fours, the leader of the pack, the alpha dog.

Andy had become…The Animal.

And all his memories of the previous night came flooding back to him in a rush…

CHAPTER TWENTY-EIGHT

The Animal experienced a quick flashback of everything that had happened the night before he woke up in a dog's kennel.

He was at Rond Point, drinking and dancing, until the last rays of sun disappeared behind the mountain and a glorious full moon took its place in the sky.

Having given up trying to break into the shriblet's cabin, the lion had left the tiger to it and gone for a walk. It found its way to Rond Point just before closing time.

"A lion!" Andy pointed, as it came into the decking area. People screamed. A stampede of ski boots stomped across the decking, fleeing for their lives. The lion roared and snapped its jaws, biting whoever couldn't run fast enough.

Andy looked on in angry disgust. "No lion attacks people in *MY* resort," he declared bravely, smashing his pint onto the ground. Perhaps it was the drink, or perhaps it was the full moon, but Andy then transformed into a werewolf. Not a pansy emo wolf like the ones in Twilight, but a full-on savage four legged monster with fangs and claws and an appetite for lion flesh. He let out a blood curdling howl, "*Aroooooooooooo!*" which was the same howl Detective Ollie and the shriblets heard several chapters ago for anyone who had been paying close attention…

Andy The Animal pounced on the lion, and an

epic battle commenced. He slashed and bit and gnawed, tasting fur and mane, and the lion retaliated. Andy's Skiworld jacket, which had somehow stayed on during the transformation, was torn to pieces, along with his trousers and t-shirt. Luckily, his pants survived the onslaught, but just as the fight was reaching a grand climax, a sharp *WHIP* cracked through the air.

The lion flinched and hesitated against the noise. Geoff, dressed as a lion tamer, snapped a big collar round the lion's neck and led him away.

The fight was over.

Some people got to their feet, staring at The Animal in awe. "You saved us!" they cheered. "Thank you, Animal!"

Andy smiled, but it looked like a snarl, and everyone ran away in terror. Everyone but a really attractive bitch. And Andy wasn't being rude, she really was a female dog, and she was giving him the eye... He knew that look, and escorted her back to her place, where they made sweet love under the moon, and the next thing Andy knew he was waking up inside the kennel the following morning.

CHAPTER TWENTY-NINE

The music blasting through the cabin was loud enough to make the walls tremble and Amy's ears pop. She couldn't resist the urge to dance, and forgot all about her grief for Phil and jumped onto the table with Hannah and Sophie. The shriblets were down to three now, but they were gonna make the bloody best of it.

Tom strode in elbow-thrusting and bobbing his head in time to the thumping bass. "Yeeeeeah!" he cried, and sauntered over to the Macarena-ing tiger. It turned to him and laid a heavy paw on his shoulder, so Tom took it in his arms and they waltzed around the room.

"This is the best party ever!" Sophie yelled, stomping on the table and shaking her hips.

"I'm so glad we found this cabin!" Hannah agreed, swaying to the rhythm.

As the music reached a crescendo, a faint rumbling began. It started soft, building slowly, ever louder until it crept above the volume of the music.

Tom twirled the tiger around and danced with it out into the snow. Icy balls were tumbling past the cabin, and suddenly he saw what was happening. The bass thumped, shaking snow off the trees, which sprinkled down around the cabin. Hannah, Sophie and Amy all stumbled out, barely keeping their feet against the rumbling mountainside.

"Oh no!" Amy pointed up the hill. "We've triggered an avalanche!"

"Good bye!" shouted the French cabin man, who leapt onto a snowmobile and sped away.

"Well, that's me done." Tom grabbed the tiger by the waist, and together they lifted off into the air, jiggling their hips in time to the music, which somehow followed them up into the sky. The shriblets were left by themselves as the mountain shook and trembled and slabs of snow skidded past their feet.

"We should go!" Hannah suggested.

"Where's our skis?!" Sophie wailed.

They were gone. All that remained was a tandem bicycle and a trailer.

Hannah and Sophie exchanged a look, and then grinned. "Yes!" They leapt onto the bike, and Amy jumped into the trailer. Hannah and Sophie counted down, "3, 2, 1, *PEDAL*!"

And they sped away from the cabin just as a massive cloud of snow obliterated it behind them.

"Aaaaaiiiieeeee!" the shriblets pedaled and shrieked as they hurtled down the mountain in front of a giant wall of tumbling snow.

CHAPTER THIRTY

Detective Ollie crept through the snowy forest, following Steph and Sue, making sure not to be seen. He was waiting for Sue to make her murderous move...

Steph stopped and her shoulders slumped. "This. Is. Hopeless." She exhaled a disgruntled sigh. "Where are all the deer?"

Sue shrugged, "Beats me." She turned to gaze around the forest, putting her back to Steph.

To Ollie's surprise, Steph then aimed a shotgun at her.

Is Steph the killer!? Ollie froze in shock.

Sue turned and saw the gun barrel pointed at her face and instinctively ducked. "What are you doing!?"

Steph followed Sue, wherever she ducked. "Hold still! There's no deer, so what else are we going to feed the signature guests?!"

"Not me!" Sue cried, squirming and moving around.

"Stop right there, murderer!"

Ollie turned to see who said that. He didn't know someone else was even there.

Steph and Sue both turned as well.

"Who are you?" asked Steph, frowning.

The stranger held out a badge and said, "Detective Oli. I've been tracking the Seasonaire Serial Killer for days, and it looks like I finally found you." He smiled a smug smile.

Utterly outraged, Ollie leapt out from behind his tree. "*NOOOOO!*" They all jumped and jerked about to face him.

"Ollie?" Sue scratched her head.

"*I'M* Detective Ollie!" Ollie jabbed his chest in emphasis. "It was *ME* who discovered the Seasonaire Serial Killer, not this…imposter!"

Steph gave a little nervous chuckle. "Ahe, guys. This is a rather big you know, misunderstanding…I'm not really a killer."

They weren't listening. Detective Oli and Detective Ollie were having an angry staring contest.

"Um, guys?" Steph asked. They didn't reply. "Okaaaay." She turned just in time to see Sue lunging for her with fangs. "What the fuck!" Steph yelped.

Sue tried to bite Steph in the neck, but she ducked in time, and then Sue turned into a bat and flapped away into the woods.

"Sue is a vampire!" Steph yelled. She gaped at Oli and Ollie, but they were locked in a silent battle of furious staring, and neither noticed.

CHAPTER THIRTY-ONE

As Sue flapped away into the woods, Steph threw her shotgun to the ground and pointed at the bat. She uttered an incomprehensible series of words and her finger started to glow red like E.T. A fireball burst from her fingertip and flew through the air.

For you see, Steph is a wizard.

The fireball hurtled towards Sue, who sensed it coming and dodged out of the way. The fireball exploded on the trunk of a tree and sputtered out while Sue fluttered into the woods.

"Dammit!" Steph cursed. She ran after Sue, leaving the two detectives engaged in their never-ending glaring contest.

Meanwhile, Garlic Matt was skiing the other way, weaving between the trees, finding peace among the calm forest. Then suddenly, a shower of burning branches and twigs rained down upon his head. "What's happening!?" he yelped. He wouldn't normally yelp, but he hadn't expected a tree to explode in front of him.

A bat flapped right into his face. "Argh!"

The bat shrieked, and transformed into a person. Matt gaped at Sue.

"*GARLIC*!" Sue yelled. "My nemesis!" Matt's breath had forced her to turn back into her human form.

Matt looked very confused. "Are you a vampire?"

"Not a vampire," Sue corrected. "I'm the countess!" She waited a while, but Matt didn't seem to get it. "You know, because I count money...I'm a countess... oh, never mind."

BOOM!

Another tree exploded and Steph's manic voice cackled through the forest. "There you are!!!"

CHAPTER THIRTY-TWO

SMASH! POW! Another rain of snowy branches fell all around Matt and Sue as Steph blasted them with her wizard powers.

"Gotta go!" Sue fled up the hill deeper into the forest.

Steph came into view, and spotted Matt lying in a heap in the snow. She calmed at the sight of him.

"Oh, hi Matt!" She beamed, forgetting her mission to obliterate Sue in an instant. Matt sometimes had that effect on girls.

"What's going on?" he asked, totally bewildered.

"Oh, you know," Steph gave a sheepish shrug. "Hunting deer. And vampires. It's turning out to be a pretty weird day…"

Matt stumbled to his feet, and was about to reply when the ground started to rumble. The distinct sound of a billion tonnes of snow tumbling down the mountain filled the air… They both slowly spun to look up the hill.

"Um…" Matt gulped. "I think that's—"

"—an avalanche!" Steph finished.

The rumbling grew to a deafening roar and the ground shook like an earthquake. Staring up the hill, they spotted something racing ahead of the wall of snow. It looked like people riding a tandem bicycle.

"*GET OUT THE WAAAAY!*" three girly voices shrieked.

The shriblets careened towards Steph and Matt, who were too stunned to move out of the way in time, and they all crashed to the floor in a messy heap underneath the bike and trailer.

Sophie and Hannah got stuck in the wheels, Amy, Steph and Matt were a tangled mess of limbs, and all of them were seconds away from snowy obliteration. The avalanche bore down on them.

"Shieldiopus!" Steph yelled.

A forcefield bubble appeared around them, just as a mighty wall of snow smashed into them. The snow flowed over and around them in a thunderous cascade. It was like being inside a safe little air pocket. The deadly snow rushed over their heads and around them and they were perfectly safe.

Matt saw the shriblets staring in awe, bewilderment spread across their confused little faces. He cocked a thumb at Steph, and said, "Turns out, she's a wizard. And Sue's a vampire. Who'd have guessed?"

CHAPTER THIRTY-THREE

Sophie and Garlic Matt's eyes met within the snowy bubble. Despite having Hannah's foot wedged under her chin and Amy's elbow in her armpit, Sophie felt nothing but the gaze of his pretty eyes.

"I can't…hold…this…anymore!" Steph wheezed. The avalanche still tumbled all around them, over their little bubble. A crack formed in the ceiling of the forcefield.

"It's gonna break!" cried Amy.

Matt saw the danger. He plucked up all of the girls within his manly arms and said, "Get ready!"

CRACK!

Steph's wizardy bubble burst and snow poured in. Matt flung everyone upwards, out of the bubble and into the air. They tumbled down the mountain, riding the avalanche on top of Matt's back like a snowboard.

Finally, everything came to a stop, and the avalanche ceased.

"We're alive!" Amy said, slightly amazed.

Hannah checked herself, and yep, all her limbs were in the right place. "Wow," she whispered.

Sophie fell to her knees and looked at the lifeless body of their heroic snowboard, Matt. "He…saved us!"

Ollie and Oli were standing in front of them, but at the sight of the random pile of Skiworld colleagues, Ollie turned and said, "Did we miss something?"

"Ha!" cried Oli, pointing. "You looked away. I win!"

Ollie glared back at him. "*NOOOO!*"

His outburst turned into a roar that seemed much louder than it should be, and continued long after he had finished speaking - *ROOOOOOOAR!*

It took a few seconds for them to realise what had made that sound. Standing a few feet away was a giant angry brown bear.

"Oh for fuck's sake, what next?" Steph said, exasperated.

And they all fled, screaming.

CHAPTER THIRTY-FOUR

Meanwhile, back in Meribel, up the hill above the town, Jack, Chris and the weird juggling unicyclist were approaching the Altiport… Also known as the Lion's Den. Quite literally, actually, because a circus had setup shop there, and taken over the runway. Tents and marquees scattered about, but what stood out the most were the cages. 12 of them in total, arranged in a circle around a central arena, and each one occupied by a snarling, angry lion.

"Great," said Chris. "How do we know which bloody lion is yours?"

"I'll know!" shrieked the juggler.

"God, this better be worth it," Jack groaned.

They approached the weird circus, and --

CRACK! The sharp sound of a whip snapped through the air rather close to Jack's head. He flinched and they all stopped on the spot.

"Who goes there?" said Geoff, finally making his proper grand entrance into the story. Naturally, he was a lion tamer because why the hell not? "You wish to enter the circus?" He eyed them all suspiciously, then brightened and beamed a welcoming smile. "5 Euros please!"

"Fuck that," said Jack. "I hate clowns."

"Yeah, we just came to get his lion back," Chris agreed.

Geoff cracked his whip again in fury. He stared

them both down. "They are *MY* lions."

They stared at him in disbelief. "Uhh, all right."

Another man approached them, wearing a top hat and a smart suit jacket. "*You* again!" He strode right up to Geoff and snatched the whip out of his hand. "I've told you to stay away! You work for Skiworld, not the circus. Now, I know the two might be very easy to confuse, but you are actually a *CHA-LAY HOST*, Mr. Wade, not a lion tamer. Now, scram!"

Geoff's head fell and he looked sad. "Okay…" And he trundled off down the hill, sniffing.

"Right, then," said Chris, rubbing his hands. "Let's get this bloody lion back so we can get paid."

CHAPTER THIRTY-FIVE

"Right, go get your lion then," Jack told the juggler.

"Ahem, not so fast," interrupted the ringleader. "If you want your lion back, you must speak to the Cube Master…follow me, please." He led them into the circus. *The Circus of Doom*.

"Don't like this one bit" commented Chris.

They came to a big tent with a square logo on a flag dangling outside. It was multi-coloured and looked like a cube…

Inside, a man with a long beard that stretched down to the ground beckoned them over.

"Greetings, Skiworld people." He bowed, even though he was sitting down. "Welcome to the Circus of Doom."

"Okay…" said Jack. He sat down in the table in front of him.

"Give this guy his lion back, and we'll be on our way," said Chris, putting on his best formal accent.

"Ha!" the man laughed. "There's only one way you'll get your lion back." He reached into his pocket and pulled out a Rubik's cube. "Whomsoever can beat me at the mightiest of challenges, can have whatever they desire."

The unicycling juggler wailed, "We're done for! No-one can beat the Cube Master!"

He wheeled about on his unicycle and went to exit the tent, when Jack put out his hand and stopped him dead in his tracks.

"Dude." He pulled the chair in closer and leaned across the table. Jack grabbed the Rubik's cube in both hands and declared, "I got this."

CHAPTER THIRTY-SIX

Jack eyed the circus man across the table, staring him down. All he had to do was complete the Rubik's cube faster than him, and he would win back the lion for the crazy unicycling juggler and earn himself a nice wad of cash.

A referee appeared at the desk and told them to, "Get ready…get set…" He paused for dramatic effect. "CUBE!"

Jack's fingers moved like lightning. In less than a second he flicked the bottom row into position. In 2 seconds, he had created a yellow T shape. From there, it was trivial. His face was pure concentration as he spun the cubes around, his fingers blurring into one. 3 seconds. Four sides of the bottom row were done.

Chris watched from behind, holding his breath. The unicycling juggler stared, utterly amazed.

4 seconds. Jack finished the 2nd row, the colours were falling into place.

5 seconds. He flicked the final row into position and spun the cube's upper row into place with a flourish. He slammed the completed Rubik's cube down onto the table.

"Yeah!!!" Chris punched the air.

"You did it!" cried the juggler.

The circus man was still struggling to get his first row into place, and when he saw Jack's cube, his mouth dangled wide open. "How did you…?"

The referee blew his whistle. "*WINNER!*" He grabbed Jack's hand and raised it into the air.

Jack smiled a smug smile, nodding his head. "Oh, yeah."

CHAPTER THIRTY-SEVEN

"I'll show them what a real Chalet Host can do…" muttered Geoff. He crept to the lion cages on the Altiport runway and made sure no-one was looking. He had a new whip and a top hat which he'd 'borrowed' from a snoozing man. He approached the nearest cage and told the lion inside, "You there."

The lion licked its lips, but remained lying on the straw of its cage, studying him with boredom, the way cats always look at humans.

Geoff cracked the whip against the bars.

The lion got annoyed by that and let out a menacing growl.

"I tame you, hairy beast of the jungle!" cried Geoff as he whipped again.

This time the lion stood up, snarling, and swung a big paw at the cage door. It rattled on its hinges.

"Yargh!" Geoff whipped again.

The lion slammed the cage door open with a mighty swipe. The rest of the lions saw what their fellow lion had done – he was free! They all swiped at their cages, breaking open the doors and suddenly Geoff found himself in the middle of a pride of angry giant cats.

"Uh oh." He turned and ran.

The unicycling juggler was patting Jack on the back, thanking him for winning his lion back, as they saw Geoff come running in the opposite direction wailing with his arms above his head.

"So mate," Chris said. "Which of these lions is…" He trailed off, unable to finish the question, because he saw what Geoff was running away from.

"Bessie!" cried the juggler in triumphant glee. But Bessie was hungry. She pounced on the juggler and swallowed him whole.

"Fuck, so much for our money!" yelled Jack, and they all turned and sprinted down the hill towards the town, chased by 12 very annoyed, very hungry lions.

CHAPTER THIRTY-EIGHT

"Mama-mia, are we a-there yet?!" Luca wheezed behind Ben as they clambered through the snow, almost to the summit of Mont Vallon.

"Just a bit further!" Ben said cheerily, full of energy.

"Why didn't we just ride the leetle floating carts?" Luca pointed to the gondola lift to their left, which Hayley and Fleur had managed to hijack earlier.

Ben didn't reply, he just kept marching on relentlessly.

At the top, Fleur and Hayley were lying beside a snowy rock, arguing in hushed whispers.

"You go first!" Fleur said.

"No, you go first!" Hayley insisted.

Fleur gave an angry sigh. "Okay, we *BOTH* go. Deal?"

Hayley chewed her lip. "Okay…"

"Ready? On 3…" said Fleur, holding up 3 fingers to make sure.

"Okay….3…"

"2…"

"1…"

"Go!" they said together, and leapt out from behind the rock.

Immy was in the dragon's nest being devoured by a dragon!

"IMMY!" they yelled in sheer horror.

The dragon looked up, its fangs dripping with goo, and gave a tiny squeaky roar.

Just then, Luca and Ben arrived. "Margarita!" shouted Luca as he tossed a pizza dough right at the baby dragon's face. It splatted across his jaws.

"What are you doing!?" cried Immy, opening her eyes. "Don't be mean to him! We were playing hide and seek! I wonder where the other 2 are hiding…"

Fleur and Hayley stared at Immy in confusion and relief. Immy looked fine, she wasn't being eaten at all.

"Are you…okay?" Hayley asked.

"Yes!" Immy said. "I'm just babysitting these little tykes."

"Babysitting!?" said Fleur.

The dragon's tongue popped through the pizza dough, licked it and sucked the whole thing into its gob. It sat there chewing noisily, then burped a little satisfied fireball.

"*TAKE THAT*!" Ben leapt out from the other side of the nest and clubbed the baby over the head with his explorer's cane.

The baby dragon yelped and went cross eyed before keeling over in an unconscious heap.

"Stop it!" Immy said. "What are you guys even doing here?"

"We are the Meribel Dragon Hunters!" Ben announced.

"We a-came to rescue you!" Luca added.

Immy just looked confused. "I don't need rescuing. But seriously, guys, you better get out of here… you shouldn't be here when –"

ROOOOOOOOAR!

"…mummy gets back," Immy finished.

The huge mother dragon swooped down and

landed on the summit. Smoke drifted from her nostrils as she leaned in and gazed at her unconscious baby. Then her eyes fell upon the intruders…

CHAPTER THIRTY-NINE

"Hreck zrruug crek?" asked the mother dragon.

"Fengik splart!" Immy replied, frantically waving her hands. She pointed to the others, who watched, confused.

The mother dragon nodded and sat down. She no longer seemed to be angry with them.

"Um...what was that?" asked Ben.

"I told her you were my friends," Immy said.

Fleur gaped. "You can speak dragon??"

"Yeah. She's French."

Hayley frowned. "That doesn't make any sense..."

Before they could question it further, the mountain rumbled.

The baby dragon squeaked in fright, and the mother looked around curiously.

"Mama mia, what is happening!" said Luca, twirling a new pizza dough above his head.

"Where do you keep getting those from?" Fleur frowned at him.

The mountain rumbled again, longer and stronger.

Hayley fell over onto her arse. "What's happening!"

The mother dragon said "Crugk ferk flunx!"

"Okay!" Immy replied. "Everyone, the mountain is going to erupt! We have to go!" She woke the baby dragon up and whispered in his ear. The baby flapped its wings and started to fly, carrying Immy with its tiny talons. Ben leapt and hugged one of the mother's big legs and Fleur quickly grabbed the other one.

"What about us!?" Hayley said. "There's no more room! Fleur, don't leave me with him!!" She pointed at Luca, still spinning a pizza with a worried look on his face.

The 2 other baby dragons came out of their hiding places behind rocks squawking and yelping in fright, flapping their tiny wings.

"Spaghetti carbonara!" cried Luca, and jumped at the yellow baby, grabbing his talons just as he took off into the sky.

Hayley ran for the green baby and did the same.

The mother flapped its huge wings and took off, carrying Fleur and Ben under her belly.

Hayley's dragon had tiny wings and couldn't fly properly. "Come on!" she encouraged. "You can do it!"

The mountain rumbled heavier and heavier now, and a deep roar came from somewhere within its bowels.

"Fly!" Hayley shouted, and finally, her baby dragon took off, just as a spurt of lava burst out of the ground of the nest.

Mother and 3 babies, each carrying the Meribel Dragon Hunters and Immy the Dragon Babysitter, into the sky. They soared upwards out of reach of the bubbling lava.

"WE'RE FLYING!" they all cried, half terrified and half overjoyed.

Then Mont Vallon blew its fiery load all over the valley in a catastrophic explosion of burning lava.

CHAPTER FORTY

"Danger from above?" Ricky said for the 34th time that day. "Danger…from…above… what could it mean?"

Laura yawned. "I don't know. As I've told you a hundred times, it's a ghost, it likes messing with us. 'Danger from above' probably doesn't mean anything."

"What if it's not though?" Ricky insisted. "It has to mean something!" He scratched his head, desperate to solve the riddle.

"Wooooo" said a spooky ghost.

"Argh!" Ricky and Laura jumped up at once. They looked around the living room, and standing by the window was the ghostly figure of…

"Phil?" Ricky said.

"Woooo! Yes! Tis meeeeeee, Phiiiiilll…" wailed Phil. "I have returnnnnnnned!"

"That's good," said Laura. "Maybe you can help us solve this ghost riddle…it wrote us a message on the Ouija board earlier this morning. It said 'danger from above.'"

Ghost Phil frowned. "How the hell should I know? I'm new to this whole being dead thing. It's kinda cool though. Check it out!" She floated into the air and flew around the room. "I can fly, and go through walls and turn invisible!" She turned invisible just to prove it. "How cool is that!?" She said from somewhere, but Ricky and Laura couldn't see her any more.

Just then, the whole house rumbled, the windows rattled and a loud *BOOM* came from somewhere in the distance outside.

Ricky ran to the window and looked out. "Fuck! Mont Vallon just erupted! *NOOOOOO!*"

"Alright, calm down," said Laura. "We're a long way away from that, we're safe here."

"*NOOOOOOOOOOO!*" Ricky shrieked, falling to his knees. "It's going to melt all the snow! How will we ski if there's no snow!?" He started to cry. The sight of the lava spraying all over the snowy mountains was too much for him to bear. He ran outside, blubbering like a baby.

"Wait, you idiot!" Laura ran (and Ghost Phil floated) out and chased after him down the hill towards the town.

CHAPTER FORTY-ONE

The grand finale approached. In real life, the Skiworld team had just survived their last ever Wednesday day off... unless you count the badasses who were staying on for an extra week because they were too cool to leave yet. Everyone else was on their way home very soon...

But that meant the story was drawing to a close, the story all about the craziest day-off in the history of ever. How would it end? Who would survive? Would we ever find out the identity of the Seasonaire Serial Killer? And numerous other unanswered questions that the writer has probably forgotten about...

Either way, there is one thing you must remember. And that is...

Life is a journey, not a destination.

The ending may excite some, it may bore others. Either way, if you have laughed, cried, smirked, giggled, or nodded thoughtfully at any moment during our brief time together... the story has fulfilled its purpose. Just as in life, we must remember and cherish the memories of the good times, and not dwell on the bad...

The end is nigh, my friends.

CHAPTER FORTY-TWO

Back in the forest, the shriblets, Steph, Sue, Ollie and Oli were running in terror from the bear that had found them.

"I'm sorry I tried to kill you!" apologized Steph to Sue.

"It's okay!" panted Sue. "I'm sorry I tried to turn you into one of my vampiric minions!"

"Run faster!" yelled Sophie, hot on the heels of Amy, who's little legs couldn't push through the snow as fast as everyone else.

"It's gaining on us!" Hannah screamed. "Steph, can't you use your wizard powers on him?"

"I can't!" Steph huffed. "I need to recharge!"

"What about you, Sue?!" Ollie suggested desperately. "You're a vampire! Can't a vampire kill a bear?"

Sue frowned as she ran. "Since when do vampires fight bears?"

"Well, it wouldn't be that weird, considering everything that's been going on…" Oli muttered.

Detective Ollie glared at his imposter. *Why are you still here?* He pondered to himself.

Just then, a mysterious figure ran out from the trees and ploughed into Oli.

The Seasonaire Serial Killer! Ollie tried to see the person's face, but he was too quick!

The figure tripped Oli up, who tumbled over his

head and sprawled out on the ground.

"Oli!" cried Steph, but it was too late. The bear pounced.

Oli was ripped to shreds in a frenzy of slashing claws, his guts spilled across the snow spraying it red and the bear ate him in 3 big bites.

"*WAAAAIIIIIII*!!!!" everyone yelled, as they sprinted as fast as they could up the hill.

Ollie couldn't contain the smirk on his face. *The killer did me a favour! When I finally catch the villain, I will thank them before putting them behind bars for good.* "Mwhahaha!" he cackled as he ran.

"What's so funny, Ollie?" Amy scolded him.

"Oh, nothing."

They ran on, heading for the town…

CHAPTER FORTY-THREE

"Hey, boss man."

"Yes beard?" Alex replied, whilst screwing in his 487th light bulb of the season.

"I got a new joke for you…"

"Ooooh," said Alex. He put down his hammer and rubbed his hands excitedly. "Do tell."

Beard bristled as he composed himself. "Why did the snowboarder cross the road?"

"I don't know," said a grinning Alex. "Why did the snowboarder cross the road?"

"To get to the other *LAVA*!!!"

Alex frowned. "Lava? That doesn't make any sen—"

His beard heaved him across the room and Alex face planted the window making a squashed expression against the glass. He peered outside and saw a steaming river of burning liquid flowing down the hill, setting fire to all of the trees and melting the snow as far as the eye could see.

"Oh my god!" Alex squealed.

He turned back to the light bulb, and desperately screwed it in.

"*WHAT ARE YOU DOING*" demanded his beard.

"I have to fix this bulb! A handyman never leaves a job unfinished."

"*FORGET THE FUCKING BULB YOU*

MORON. WE ARE ABOUT TO BE BURNED ALIIIIVE." His beard yanked him out the door and down the stairs. The lava poured over Mottaret, melting the metal snowman, which bent and buckled before tipping over into the burning river.

"*STOP STANDING THERE AND BOARD, BOARD FOR YOUR LIFE BOSS MAN!*"

Alex strapped into his snowboard and hurtled under the tunnel towards the Trout run. Mottaret was consumed by the lava, and the entire village went up in flames.

He sped down the slope in front of the bubbling, boiling, deadly flow of lava. He was screaming in terror, but other than that he looked like quite the hero.

The Chaudanne came into view and Alex spotted a gathering of familiar faces all yelling and arguing with each other.

It was the rest of the Skiworld crew.

CHAPTER FORTY-FOUR

"It was the Seasonaire Serial Killer!" shrilled Detective Ollie. "He came out of nowhere and murdered Oli!"

"You are insane!" cried Amy.

"It was YOU!" pointed Sue. "You threw Oli to the bear! We saw you do it!"

"Me?!" Ollie said in disbelief. "I have been hunting down the nefarious killer in our midst ever since I got here! He has been picking us off one by one, how have you not noticed!?"

"You lunatic!" said Sophie. "They didn't die…they went *HOME*!"

"What?" Ollie's eyes went wide.

"Nobody died until this crazy ridiculous day started!" Steph screamed.

Alex skidded to a halt in front of them. "Guys! Why are you just standing here at the bottom of the Chaudanne? Have you not seen the *LAVA* heading this way?"

"The snoooow," wept Ricky.

"We have to get out of here!" said Alex.

"But there's lions back that way!" yelled Chris, pointing up the road.

"And a hungry bear!" added Hannah, pointing to the trees.

"And a perverted ghost!" added Laura, pointing up the hill.

"And that's a dragon!" added Amy, pointing at the sky.

"And a dog dog..." added Jack.

Everyone flapped their arms in the air. "*WE'RE SURROUNDED!*"

CHAPTER FORTY-FIVE

Jack, Chris, Amy, Sophie, Hannah, Steph, Sue, Geoff, Ollie, Ghost Phil, Laura, Ricky and Alex huddled at the bottom of the Chaudanne, drawn together by all manner of crazy shit that had been going down that day.

The distant roar of lions, dragons and that random bear grew steadily louder. The sizzle of burning lava filled the air in the other direction. There was nowhere to go.

From the mountains, the sound of dogs suddenly overcame everything else. They turned as one in time to see a ferocious-looking wolf bounding out of the trees followed by a pack of dogs all different shapes and sizes, yapping and barking.

The wolf bounded right at them.

"AAAAIIIGHhh— huh?" everyone started to scream but cut off when the wolf stood up on 2 legs and turned into Andy.

"Hi, everyone!" he said with a little wave. "You wouldn't believe the day I'm having…"

They all just stared at him.

"Danger from above…" Ricky muttered.

"The day *YOU'RE* having?" Steph put her hands on her hips. "This is the *WORST* day ever!"

"Danger from above…" Ricky repeated. He jabbed Laura in the arm. "He's our boss… the ghost was trying to warn us about Andy! He's the danger!"

Laura gaped. It all suddenly made sense.

"Dangerous? Me?" Andy frowned. "No!" He chuckled nervously. "This is just one of those really bad days. It happens every season, man!"

"We're all going to die!" Ollie wailed.

"Pfft," Andy gave a dismissive wave. "Days like this, when all shit seems to be going wrong, that's when you find your superpower. Turns out I'm a werewolf! How cool is that!"

"Um, guys?" Sue said, pointing towards the town.

The pride of angry lions spilled from the road and spread out in a hunting formation. Slowly, they stalked towards the huddle of terrified Skiworld friends.

"Well, it was nice knowing ya," Ricky said.

"This is the doggest of dog days, man," Jack groaned.

Andy's pack of mutts barked wildly. "Alright, alright, boys," Andy said to them, and they calmed. "Well, I'm going in. Anyone else feel like kicking the shit out of this ridiculous day, find your Seasonaire Super Power and join me! *YOU WANT SOME, KITTY?*" He howled at the sky, transformed into a wolf, and charged at the nearest lion. His minions followed, all barking and biting, attacking the lions and scattering them.

"He is The Animal," said Alex, awed.

The river of lava poured out of the Trout run, heading right for them.

"The snowwww!" Ricky burst into tears again.

"*STAND BACK*," declared Alex, in a very beard-like voice. "*I WILL SAVE YOU ALL.*"

CHAPTER FORTY-SIX

Alex's beard started to grow. It sprouted from his chin and expanded like a hedge, growing out and out and creeping across the snow like a big ginger bush. It grew to over ten feet tall and a hundred feet wide, a giant sprawling mass of bristly hairs and vines, forming a barricade. The lava flowed into it, but could not go any further. The beard sizzled and steamed, but more hairs kept growing out of Alex's chin, replacing the singed ones, and stopping the lava dead in its tracks.

"Alex…" stared Ricky, who finally stopped crying when he saw what was happening. "Alex is saving the snow! Alex is Beard Man!"

Then *ZOMBIES* started climbing up out of the ground. Dead hands heaved themselves up and within moments, the Skiworld crew were surrounded by a horde of the undead.

"This is getting so *OUT OF HAND*!" yelled Steph. "It's time to end this!" She lifted her finger into the air and summoned a mighty bolt of lightning, zapping a zombie to smithereens.

Sue morphed into a vampire bat and flapped into the sky, attacking the closest zombie she could find. She clutched him by the ears and yanked his head off.

Detective Ollie pulled out his twin six-shooters, laughing hysterically and blasting heads off.

"Yeaaaah!" cried the rest of the team, feeling inspired.

"Fuck it man, let's get stuck in yeah?" Chris said to

Jack.

"Yeah man," Jack replied, grabbing a ski pole and the two of them charged into the fray.

Geoff ran into the zombies cracking his whip, flicking limbs off in every direction.

Laura and Ricky put both sets of skis across their shoulders and spun like a deadly windmill, spinning wildly and cutting the zombies clean in half.

The enormous dragon swooped down from the sky, carrying Ben and Fleur in its talons. "Attack!" they ordered the mother dragon, who obeyed. She dive bombed, raining her fiery breath onto the horde of zombies.

"That's a spicy meat-a-ball!" cried Luca, cackling with glee as he dangled from the claws of his baby dragon.

Hayley soared in behind him, her own baby dragon spitting fire onto the zombies.

"Team Shriblets Unite!" Amy sprayed lemon into the zombie's eyes to blind them so Hannah and Sophie could kick off their heads in perfect ninja synchronisation and Ghost Phil floated around making scary ghost noises.

"PAR-TAY TIME!" came a call from the sky, and Tom floated into the battle with his dancing tiger. Pumping music filled the air as the Chaudanne turned into a chaotic version of the Folie Douce, just with less tables and more blood, carnage and mayhem.

A stray fireball flew into the roof of the ESF building, and soon the whole structure was a raging inferno.

But it didn't matter. The Skiworld team were fighting back, like true heroes. If anyone could save the town, it was them.

CHAPTER FORTY-SEVEN

The Battle for Meribel came to an end at last.

Standing victorious in the Chaudanne, the Skiworld team surveyed the carnage that lay before them. Dead zombies littered the ground, the town was on fire, and most of the snow had melted. Flowers sprouted amid the green grass, signifying that spring was on the way…

They had survived.

Chris yanked the handle of a ski pole out of a dead zombie's skull and slung it over his shoulder. "We did it." He nodded to Jack, who was sitting on the ground, lighting a roll up.

"Yeah, we did."

Immy reached up to the mother dragon, who was purring softly as she scratched under her chin. "Take care of them!" Tears fell from the corners of Immy's eyes, as the baby dragons each licked Fleur, Hayley, Ben and Luca's hands. They would forever be friends. The dragons flapped their wings and swooped into the sky, searching for a new home.

Hannah and Sophie sat with their heads on each other's shoulders, contemplating how awesome it was to be alive.

Luca walked amid the battlefield, videoing the aftermath, and offering pizza to the hungry combatants.

Andy The Animal came over to where the team

were standing. He transformed into a human again and spoke. "Guys! We did it. The town may be on fire, and we may have accidentally destroyed it with our super powers and our dragons, but never mind about any of that! We have survived. Remember this day, because Meribel will never forget us!"

And with that, he morphed back into a wolf, and bounded away with his dog lover and the rest of his pack.

A stunned silence filled the air. The Skiworld team looked at one another, and knew their lives had changed forever. They were no longer the same person that started this adventure, they were something much more now.

It had been the craziest, most ridiculous, batshit insane day off... but also one of the best. A real adventure.

Tom looked up at the sky and saw a twinkling star disappear. It was probably his space ship, leaving without him. But he didn't mind. "Think I'll stay here," he said, looking around at his friends. He belonged here, with his true people. "I think it's party time!"

The sun set behind the mountain. All that remained was to enjoy this night and look forward to what could happen tomorrow...

THE END

A NOTE FROM THE AUTHOR

Well, that sure got out of hand fast. Thank you for reading this nonsensical tale of ridiculousness, and let it be a hopelessly inaccurate memento of all the experiences we had during our time in Meribel.

I am, of course, talking to my 28 Skiworld co-workers and friends, without whom, this story could not have existed. If, for some reason, you *aren't* one of those 28 people, but have bought this book anyway… Well, I can only apologise and wonder what in God's name possessed you to do that. But I thank you as well.

I was supposed to finish my second novel while out here, but I've ended up spending a worrying amount of time putting this together instead. Do I regret it? Nah. The best cure for writer's block is to write something completely different, and this has proven to be a very worthwhile antidote.

For now, this is farewell. But I hope we meet again.

M A Clarke,
April 2015

ABOUT THE AUTHOR

M A Clarke is a 29 year old geek from England who
grew up watching cartoons, animating his own
cartoons, and playing video games. He recently
decided to explore the world and see what life was
like away from a screen. Rather ironically, travelling
inspired him to sit in front of a screen and write his
first novel, *Lunaria,* which you can check out at
lunarianovel.com.
He has a dangerous addiction to Wispa chocolate bars
and also loves mountains, dogs, dinosaurs and space.
You might like his website: www.mattclarke.co.uk